At the top of a very tall hill in a very small place called Woollybottom is a horseshoe of houses.

And in those houses live six BEST friends, including a bunny called Benjamin Bounce.

Charlie's house

Walter's house

Winnie's house

Winnie's Workshop

Polly's house

The Wishing well

Benjamin Bounce's house

Chloe's house

The pond

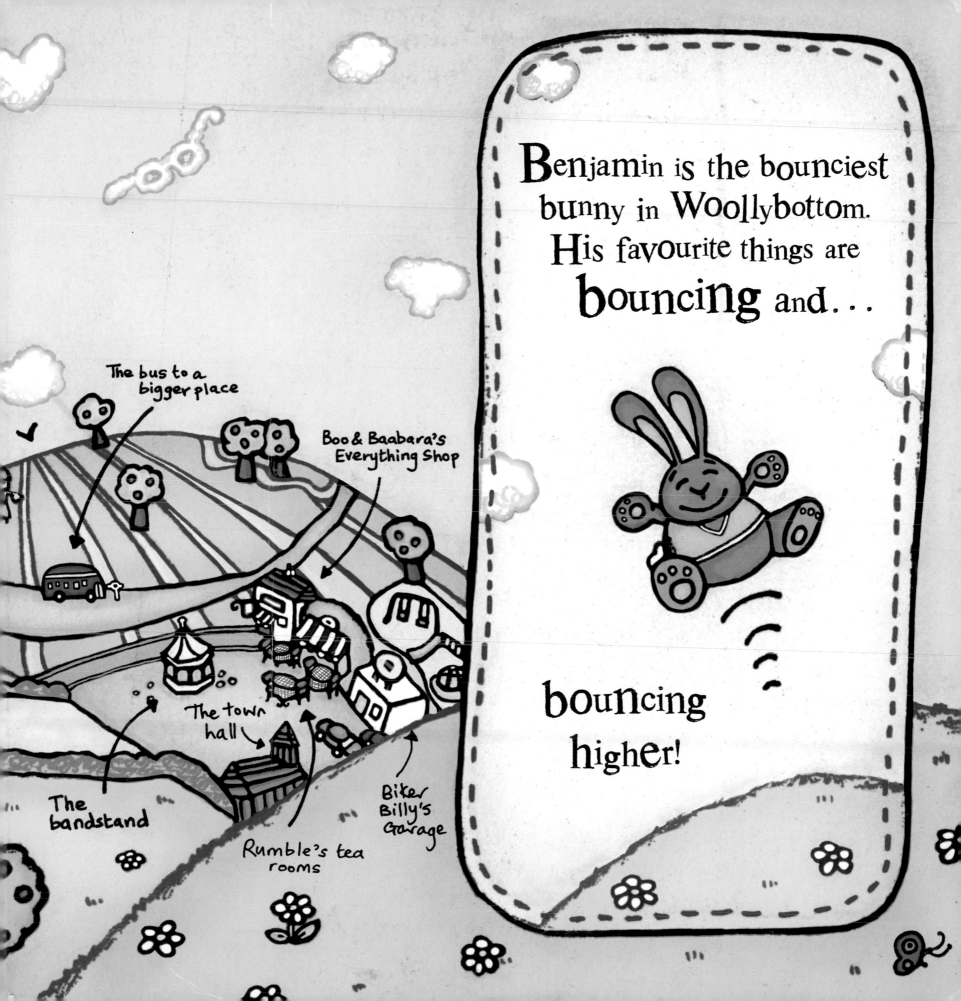

Benjamin is the bounciest bunny in Woollybottom. His favourite things are **bouncing** and...

bouncing higher!

The bus to a bigger place

Boo & Baabara's Everything Shop

The town hall

The bandstand

Rumble's tea rooms

Biker Billy's Garage

Yes,
Benjamin
is full of
beans.
He just
never stops
bouncing.

But this story is about the time
when Benjamin's bounce
got him into
a bit of trouble.

And it all started
with a very
big...

'Ooops, sorry,' he said. 'I didn't see you there.'

'Perhaps you need glasses, Benjamin?' said Polly.

'OOF! NO THANKS!' said Benjamin,
who couldn't think of anything worse.

'I don't need glasses. And anyway, they'd
get in the way of my bouncing.'

But Benjamin didn't
want to be the only
one in Woollybottom
with glasses,
so he just kept
on bouncing...

until he went...

THUD!

into a hole in the ground, where he got
completely and utterly wedged.

'Mffmmtomorrmfffl,' said Benjamin.

'I THINK he said maybe he SHOULD
go for an eye test tomorrow, after all,' said Walter.

All the
Woollybottomers
agreed.

The very next day, Benjamin plucked up the courage to go to the Opticians and all his friends went with him.

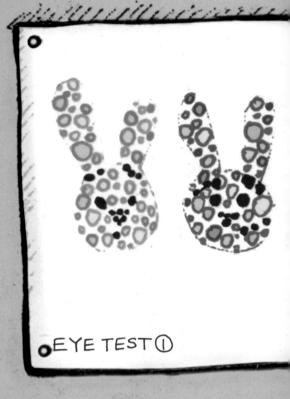

EYE TEST ①

With knots in his tummy, he did his best, but . . .

Benjamin DID need glasses! And he was the only one!
The only one in **Woollybottom** who looked different.

Not only that, but he couldn't do any bouncing either, because that just made his glasses fall off.

He'd never be able to have FUN again!

'Oh!' cried Benjamin, steaming up.
'I HATE having glasses!'

Luckily, his friends weren't far away.

'Don't worry,' said Winnie, 'We'll help...
Can we borrow them?'

'With pleasure!' said Benjamin.
'I need to catch up with my bouncing!'

And so off went the
Woollybottomers
to Winnie's
Workshop.

Winnie's
Workshop

BUSY

NIGHT
VISION
YEAH!

3D YOUR LIFE

Together they came up with
an INGENIOUS plan.

They twiddled and tweaked,
added and improved, and did all
kinds of things to the glasses.

X-RAYING
STUFF UP
FOR DUMMIES

SUPER-
FICATION
1.Take
Ordinary
Spectacles

2.Apply
Genius

3.Believe
to
See

Until at last they had created . . .

BENJAMIN'S
BRAND-NEW-
HARDLY-
RECOGNISABLE-
SUPER-
SPECTACLES!

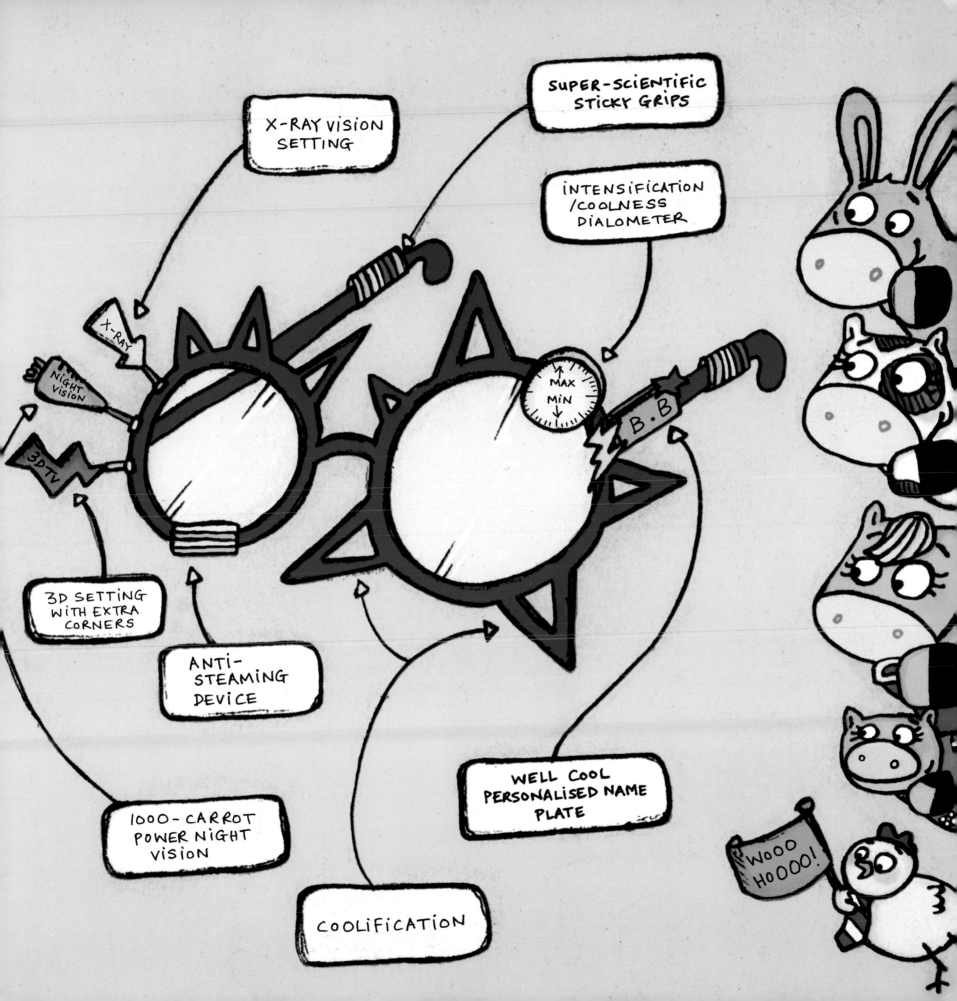

He was **SO** excited,
he started **bOuncing!**

And guess what?

Thanks to the

SUPER-SCIENTIFIC STICKY GRIPS,

the spectacles stayed
completely ON!

Not only that, but they had
an AMAZING X-RAY setting . . .
Benjamin couldn't believe his eyeballs!

Oh, how the
Woollybottomers blushed!

In fact, the spectacles were
so BRILLIANT that
EVERYONE wanted some.
NOT wearing glasses was
BORING!

Walter and Winnie decided there was only one thing for it . . .

They worked all night long, plotting and planning and preparing for the **amazing**, the **marvellous**, the **SUPER**. . .

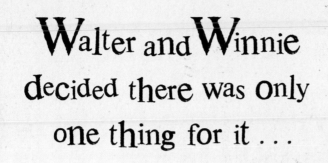

MASTERPLAN

WOO HoOo!

WOOLLYBOTTOM

Woollybottom Specs-tacular!

You see, what this story is really about is the time when Benjamin realised that being different is what you make it . . .

SEE THE WORLD ANEW!

WOO HOO!

THE WOOLLYBOTTOM WEEKLY TRUMPET

FREE

NEWS FROM A LOVELY PLACE

GLASSES CRAZE SWEEPS WOOLLYBOTTOM

JOURNAMOLE EXCLUSIVE SCOOP BENJAMIN BOUNCE'S BOUNCINESS HAS BEEN CONTAGIOUS IN WOOLLYBOTTOM THIS WEEK. EVERYONE'S ROCKING THE GLASSES LOOK. IT'S SPECS-TACULAR!

NEXT WEEK IN WOOLLYBOTTOM:

SPORTS & FUNDAY ON SUNDAY!

For all those who have helped me see that life is, in fact, one long Specs-tacular.

& with special love for my wonderful family & for Mandy & Helen.

First published in paperback in Great Britain by HarperCollins Children's Books in 2013
1 3 5 7 9 10 8 6 4 2
ISBN: 978-0-00-744550-9
HarperCollins Children's Books is a division of HarperCollins Publishers Ltd.
Text and illustrations copyright © Rachel Bright 2013
The author/illustrator asserts the moral right to be identified as the author/illustrator of this work.
A CIP catalogue record for this title is available from the British Library. All rights reserved.
No part of this publication may be reproduced, stored in a retrieval system, or transmitted in any form or by
any means, electronic, mechanical, photocopying, recording or otherwise, without the prior permission of
HarperCollins Publishers Ltd. 77-85 Fulham Palace Road, Hammersmith, London W6 8JB.
Visit our website at: www.harpercollins.co.uk
Printed and bound in China